Marvellous Manners

Princesses
Love To
Share!

Timothy Knapman

Illustrated by **Jimothy Oliver**

QED Publishing

Polly wanted to be a **princess**,
she wore a **golden crown** in her hair.

She had lots of **toys**, which she kept to herself, because:

"**Princesses don't share!**"

She had plenty of games, a great big TV,
and look at that **beautiful dress!**

But no one could come near any of it:
"They'd **just** make a **terrible mess!**"

Her garden was an **adventure park**
with all kinds of slides and swings.

But she wouldn't allow people to use it:
"They'd only **ruin my things!**"

Polly's new friend was **Chloe**,
she was **all** that a friend should be.

Polly thought she could be **trusted**,
so she **asked** her over for tea.

Dear Chloe,
please .

Polly spent **days** getting ready,
she'd waited for so **very long**.

Then Chloe arrived at last, and,
oh dear...
that's when the whole thing went wrong!

Chloe cried, "What a beautiful **dolly**!"
Then she **grabbed it**
and **played** with it, too!

She **played** all the games
and she **watched** the TV.
Polly didn't know what to do!

The next Polly knew, Chloe put on **that** dress, and said, **"Let's go play outside!"**

And then Chloe fell - **splat!** - in a puddle
when she **flew** off the end of the slide.

Once Chloe had gone, Polly looked at her things –
they'd been **played with** and **ruined**
and **touched!**

They took ages to put right and poor Polly cried,
"Never again!
It's too much!"

For **days** Polly sat in her house with her things –
she was **lonely** and **sad**, as you see.

Till one day a **letter** from Chloe arrived saying,
"Polly, oh **please** come to tea."

Polly ran all the way, she'd **missed** Chloe so much!
Chloe said, "We've got **plenty to do.**

"Look at the toys and the games we can **share**,
they'll be twice as much **fun** now we're **two!**"

So Polly was **happy**, at very long last,
which was, after all, only fair.

Princesses have plenty, but never have fun
till they realize they do **love to share**.

Next steps

Ask your child what they know about princesses. Do they know where they live, what they look like or what they wear?

Talk about the different types of toys that your child has recently seen or played with.

Ask your child why they think Polly kept all her toys to herself and why she did not allow anyone to come near any of them. Talk about how Polly might feel if she continued to think and behave this way about her toys.

Can your child remember the name of Polly's friend? Discuss what her friend (Chloe) did when she arrived at Polly's house. Ask your child how Chloe felt about sharing things. How does this compare to how Polly feels about sharing? Do you have any ideas why these two girls might feel differently?

Why does your child think Polly felt lonely and sad?

Talk about what eventually made Polly feel happy. Can your child describe the picture on the last page? Make sure your child understands that sharing their toys with their friends can be more fun than playing alone.

After reading the story together, ask your child how they feel when they play alone and how they feel when they play with their friends. Who does your child like to share their toys with?

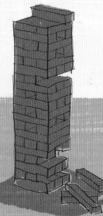

Consultant: Cecilia A. Essau
Professor of Developmental
Psychopathology
Director of the Centre for Applied
Research and Assessment in Child and
Adolescent Wellbeing, Roehampton
University, London

Editor: Alexandra Koken
Designer: Andrew Crowson

Copyright © QED Publishing 2012
First published in the UK in 2012 by
QED Publishing
A Quarto Group company
230 City Road
London EC1V 2TT

www.qed-publishing.co.uk

A catalogue record for this book is available from the British Library.

ISBN 978 1 84835 898 0

Printed in China